ACROSS
THE
RAINBOW
BRIDGE

For Catherine Fisher
with love and
admiration
KC-H

For Gwyneth,
Arthur, and
Owain
JAL

KEVIN CROSSLEY-HOLLAND
illustrated by JEFFREY ALAN LOVE

ACROSS THE RAINBOW BRIDGE

STORIES OF NORSE GODS AND HUMANS

CANDLEWICK STUDIO
an imprint of Candlewick Press

CONTENTS

Foreword vi

The Troll and the Trickster 1

Skarp's Ghost 25

Blue of Blue 41

Your Life or My Life 59

The Gift of Poetry 75

FOREWORD

Just over one thousand years ago, the rulers of Iceland decided that their island should officially become Christian. But they also wisely said that if any Icelanders preferred to go on worshipping the old gods, they could do so in private.

For centuries, the people living in the countries that we now call Scandinavia (Iceland, Norway, Sweden, and Denmark) had worshipped the gods who lived in Asgard, a world high above the earth. And they believed that these gods sometimes crossed a three-strand rainbow bridge and came down to Midgard (Middle Earth), the world inhabited by human beings, giants, and dwarfs.

More than once, the god Thor rode down in his sky-chariot, drawn by goats, to do battle with the giants. The trickster Loki came down to do a shady deal with the greedy dwarfs and to rescue a goddess. Hermod came down on his way to the misty, freezing world of Niflheim, nine days' ride northward and downward from Midgard.

And many gods came for the sheer joy of seeing Middle Earth throw off her gray-and-white winter clothing and put on a coat of summer colors.

From time to time the gods crossed the rainbow bridge to help human beings—most of them stay-at-home farming families, who fished, grew their crops, and tended their livestock in a harsh environment while some of their daring young sons (the men we call Vikings) sailed east, south, and west and raided, traded, and even settled in Russia, the British Isles, and much of mainland Europe, Greenland, and Newfoundland. (No one, incidentally, is completely sure what the word *Viking* actually means. The most likely translation is "a Scandinavian abroad.")

So one tale in this book tells how Loki managed to outwit a dangerous troll threatening to kidnap a child. Another tells how the goddess Frigg first taught a girl to grow flax and make linen, "cool in summer and warm in winter—the finest of all fabrics."

The Scandinavians knew that they shared Middle Earth with all kinds of supernatural beings. Not only were there dwarfs living in crannies and caves, but frost-giants and rock-giants like Vafthrudnir (Tangler), who took part in a deadly riddle contest with a one-eyed stranger. Ghosts and specters were here, there, and everywhere, and so were hobgoblins and terrifying sendings—corpses brought to life by magicians and sent on deadly missions. For the most part these spirits lived peacefully side by side with human beings, but if people disrespected them, there was a price to pay.

People thought that those who had wrongly suffered in their lives, or who were misers, were unable to sleep quietly in their graves. They believed their ghosts walked at night, like the farmer Skarp's ghost. But they also thought that a man or woman who had just died could pass on a precious gift to a living boy or girl, as the poet Halldor does in the moving last story in this book.

These rural tales were mostly written down in Iceland after what is known as the Viking Age, the period between the early ninth and late eleventh centuries. Look closely now. What makes them so blood-bright and so relevant today is what underlies and drives them. They assert the great importance of family and of equal partnership between men and women. They demonstrate the value of true friendship, hard work, having a dream, and having a sense of humor too. They tell us to face up to our greatest fears and to be brave when it's not so easy to be. They awaken us to the sheer beauty of the physical world and quicken us to the joy of being alive.

Kevin Crossley-Holland,
Chalk Hill, October 2020

THE
TROLL
AND THE
TRICKSTER

———

Some things are very bad.
Trolls are worse.

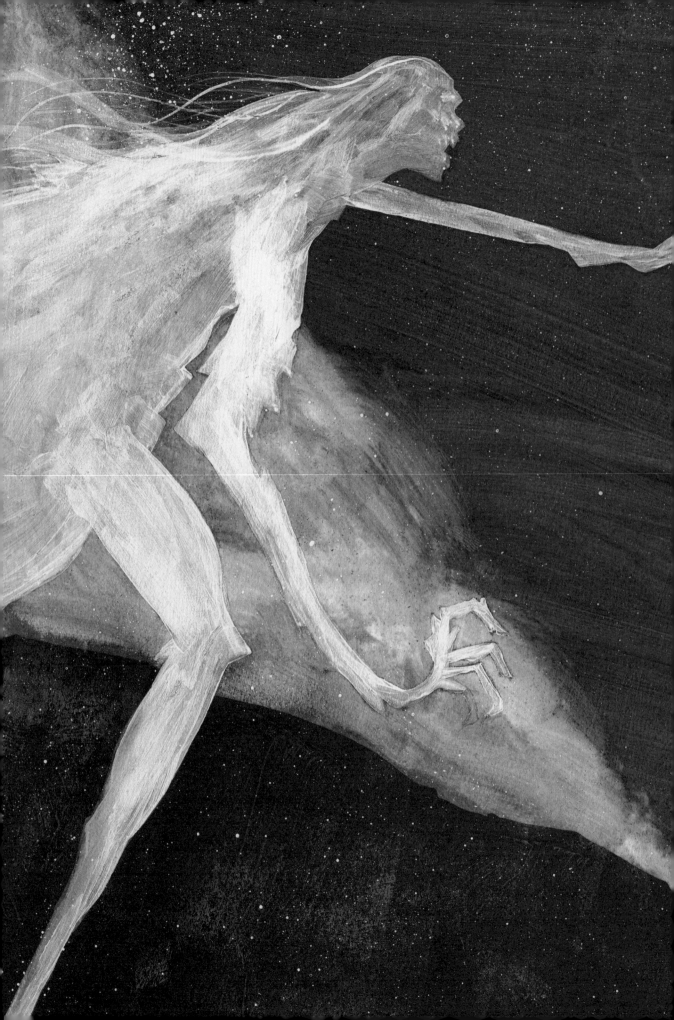

How could it be?

But it could.

After a mellow, yellow August afternoon, the north wind could get up all of a sudden and sweep over the glacier, across the scrub and the scruffy pasture, and down to Ulf and Thora's longhouse, and if they or their little daughter, Asta, were out and about without their hoods or oilskins, it could stiffen their bones so that they staggered back indoors, stiff-legged, like walking skeletons.

That was when trolls went on the prowl and ghosts went walking, and there was nothing for it but to sprinkle fresh water on the threshold, bolt the door, and hope for the best.

Some days Asta fished for herring and cod with her father, but they never ventured so far out that the fearsome Midgard Serpent could rise from the depths and snaffle them. Some days she helped her mother to milk their three cows and feed them sweet hay. When he was born, her baby brother turned out to be a sad little thing, a mewing weakling, and her parents had left him up on the glacier. So Asta was their only child, and they never let her out of their sight.

In the evenings, Ulf rather liked to play a board game or two—fox and geese, or draughts. Sometimes he played with Asta, sometimes with a neighbor, though the nearest lived a mile and more away.

One late August evening, when the days were already getting so much shorter and the bitter north wind was rollicking round their longhouse, there was a knocking at the door.

"Who's there?" Ulf called out.

"Me."

"Who's me?"

"Open the door or I'll knock it down," barked the voice.

So Ulf unbolted the door, and there stood a mountain-troll, and he wasn't a small one.

The troll bent at the waist, lowered his head, and pushed through the door into the fire hall.

"That's better," he growled. "It's blue-cold outside."

Then he peered down at Asta and little Asta stared up at him. And when she saw how ugly he was, with a nose like a purple pumpkin, and strings of snot hanging from each nostril, and how he couldn't even stand upright without bumping his head on the roof beam, she felt more sorry for him than scared of him.

"Don't just gape, girl," her father told her. "Go and pour our guest some milk or ale."

"Ale," said the mountain-troll, and he slapped his stomach and clapped his coarse hands.

Thora stood up from her loom. "I'll go and get some bread and cheese," she said.

The troll wiped his nose on his sleeve and stared around him.

"Ah! You can play board games, can you?"

"Why?" replied Ulf. "Can you?"

"Certainly," said the troll. "What stakes shall we play for?"

"Me," said Ulf, "I usually play for a coin or two."

The troll grunted. "I say . . . whoever wins can ask the loser for one of his possessions. He can ask for whatever he wants."

Ulf lowered his eyes. *If I lose,* he thought, *well, Thora and I are so poor we have little this troll would want. But if I win, I'll ride over to wherever he lives and take my pick . . .*

"Well?" demanded the troll.

"Agreed," said Ulf, and with that the two of them sat down on the huge split log beside the firepit with the gaming board between them. They arranged the wooden pegs and began to play the game of fox and geese.

They played for one hour, they played for two. And sitting on a wooden tub, Asta watched them.

Outside, the north wind was bumping and blundering into the turf walls of the longhouse, but in the fire hall it was comfy and warm. The wax candles scarcely trembled and the peat in the fire smelled sweet. Asta listened to the clicking and threshing of her mother's loom, she stared at the bone pieces until they shone in the gloom and came alive, she heard the troll sniffing and snorting or from time to time muttering—"Hmm! . . . No! . . . No, better not . . . What a disaster!"—and she began to drowse, then to dream.

Late into the night, the troll knew that Ulf was beaten. He polished off his ale, slapped his stomach again, and began to chuckle.

"A good game," said Ulf. "I must admit, if I hadn't seen it with my own eyes, I wouldn't have believed a fellow as huge and hefty as you could be so neat and nimble with all the little pegs."

"Or so sharp-witted," added the troll. "Well, I'm the winner . . . What did you say your girl's name is?"

"I didn't," said Ulf.

"I choose her," announced the troll, and he guffawed. "I choose your daughter."

"No, no, you can't," Ulf protested, and then Thora woke up and joined in. The two of them got down on their knees and put their hands over their hearts and begged the troll.

"She's the life of our lives," they pleaded. "She's our future."

"A deal's a deal," grunted the troll.

He looked down at sobbing Thora and then at Asta, still sleeping under her sheepskin.

"I'll tell you what," he said. "You can keep her for one more night. Until tomorrow at midday. And if you can hide her so well that I can't find her, you can keep her for good. But if I can find her, I'll take her away."

Then the mountain-troll laughed in their faces, unbolted the door himself, and stumped out into the night.

Ulf and Thora thought of all the places where they might hide their golden daughter, but there wasn't a single one where they could be sure the troll wouldn't find her.

"Pray to the water-spirit who helped you give birth to Asta," her husband pleaded.

But his wife shook her head. "She's only a spirit. I'll pray to Odin himself. I'll beg Allfather to come and help us."

So Thora and Ulf got down on their knees and implored the greatest of all the gods to come and help them. Then they lay down beside the dozing fire with their daughter between them.

But they hadn't been asleep for long before there was a knocking so loud that the poor door shook in its frame.

Thora and Ulf both sat up.

"It's the troll," gasped Thora.

"No," said her husband. "It's not even daybreak yet."

Their visitor was wearing a wide-brimmed hat and a midnight-blue cloak

and carrying a spear that shone in the moonlight. He had only one eye.

Ulf and Thora recognized him at once and fell forward onto their knees.

"Give me your daughter," Allfather instructed them. "I'll hide her so the troll will never find her."

And what Odin did was to chant a spell over Asta and change her into a single blade of grass. Then he walked out of the fire hall and hid the blade in the grassy pasture next to the longhouse.

"Your daughter will be safe there," Odin assured her parents. "I'll watch over her."

Well, day soon dawned, and at midday the troll barged into the longhouse. He didn't even bother to greet Ulf and Thora.

"Where is she?" he demanded. "I'll soon find her. I'll soon have her."

The troll had a quick look round the fire hall and the cowshed and then in the creaky wooden haybarn.

"No," he growled. "Outside, then."

The troll turned north; he turned south, east, and west. And then, as surely as a water diviner can find a fresh spring, he turned to the pasture of long grass.

"Give me a sickle," he ordered Ulf.

Ulf shook his head.

"You heard me," snarled the troll.

First he cut down half of Ulf's precious grass, grabbing one fistful after another, glaring at it and throwing it over his right shoulder. But then he picked out a single blade . . .

Ulf and Thora were watching, and Thora couldn't help herself. She began to tremble.

Odin was watching too. He was hiding behind a little wooden fence and had made a hole right through it with his spear, as if it were an auger, and put his one eye to it.

Then Allfather filled his lungs and blew the grass blade out of the troll's grasp. Odin blew it straight back to Thora, and the moment she caught it, the blade turned straight back into her sweet daughter.

"What I can do," Ulf heard Allfather say, "I have done. But the time comes when here on Middle Earth each man must help himself and each woman help herself."

And with that, Odin disappeared.

But the troll followed Ulf and Thora and their daughter to the door of the longhouse.

"Very clever!" he scoffed. "But you'll have to be more cunning than that if you want to keep your daughter. I'll be back at midday tomorrow and I'll find where you've hidden her."

All afternoon and evening, Ulf and Thora were uneasy, wondering what they could do. Now and then they thought of a place to hide their daughter, only to dismiss it.

"That troll was able to find a single grass blade . . ." Ulf began. "So . . . so . . ."

"Let's pray to Honir," his wife suggested. "He's a peacemaker."

Ulf sniffed. "Honir! His legs are as long as a stork's and he never makes his mind up. That's all I know about him."

While Asta slept, the farmer and his wife got down on their knee bones and prayed, and when Thora unbolted their door next morning, shining Honir was standing there.

"Give me your daughter," he instructed them. "I'll hide her so the troll will never find her."

So Ulf and Thora gave their daughter to the god, and what he did was change her in front of their eyes into a little quartz pebble. Then Honir stalked along the stream running past the longhouse down to the sea and planted the pebble among the millions of other shining quartz pebbles on the beach.

Well, at midday the troll barged in again, and no sooner in than out. He turned north; he turned south, east, and west. And then, as surely as a water diviner can find a fresh spring, he turned to the beach.

Thora began to tremble.

The troll prowled up and down, up and down. He picked up fistful after fistful of pebbles, and then he found the one he was searching for.

Honir was watching, and he took pity on Ulf and Thora and their daughter. He filled his lungs and blew the tiny pebble out of the troll's hands and up to the longhouse, and there it turned back into the girl again.

"What I can do I have done," shining Honir told them. "But now you must help yourselves."

And with that, Honir stalked away.

"Very clever!" snorted the troll. "But not crafty enough. I'll be back tomorrow at midday. Wherever you hide her, I'll find her, and this time I won't spare you."

All that night, Ulf and Thora were unable to sleep.

The north wind was resting, and in the longhouse it was so quiet that they could hear wood ash shifting and settling on ash, and Asta sighing softly in her sleep.

"We could pray to Loki," Thora said in a listless voice.

"Loki!" exclaimed Ulf. "Why not Thor? He'd frighten the troll away."

Thora shook her head. "Loki comes down to Midgard more often than the other gods . . . and he loves to show just how clever he is."

"That's true!" her husband agreed. "He rescued Odin and shining Honir from that magician."

Then Ulf and his wife got down on their knees and prayed to the Trickster, and scarcely had they done so than he was standing right beside them, flickering and orange.

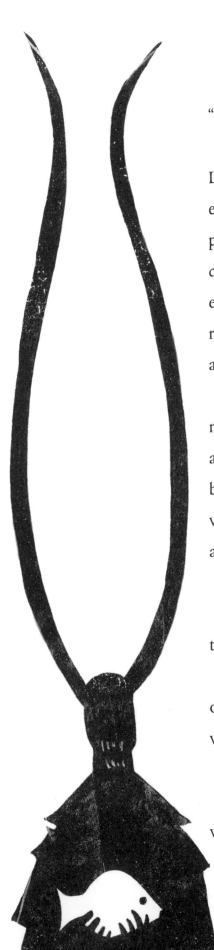

"Give me your little daughter," he bragged. "I'll hide her so this troll will never, ever find her."

So Ulf and Thora gave their daughter to Loki, and there and then he turned her into an egg, no larger than a grain, glistening in the palm of his right hand. The Trickster bounded down to the foreshore, caught a flounder, and embedded this egg among her roe. Then he released the squirming fish and she swam away as fast as she could.

When he came back the next day, the mountain-troll wasted very little time in looking around the fire hall, the cowshed, and the hay-barn. He turned north; he turned south, east, and west. And then, surely as a water diviner can find a fresh spring, he turned to the salty sea.

Ulf and Thora lowered their eyes.

"Lend me your boat and tackle," growled the troll.

But as Ulf helped the troll drag the boat out of the tumbledown boatshed and down to the water, Loki walked up to them.

"Who are you?" asked the troll.

"Oh! Just a neighbor!" Loki replied with a wave of his right hand. "Going fishing, are you?"

"What does it look like?" the troll replied.

17

"I'll come with you."

"As you like," grunted the troll.

When the troll and Loki had rowed from the shore, they lowered their lines and began to fish. Each time the troll caught a fish, he checked it and then chucked it back into the water.

"Farther out," he growled.

"Not too far," Loki warned him. "You've heard about the Midgard Serpent."

The mountain-troll sniffed.

"We'd make a nice tasty meal," Loki said, "the two of us."

But then the troll caught the flounder, unhooked her, and dropped her at his feet, squirming and flapping. At once he began to row back to land.

When he had beached Ulf's little boat, he quickly cut the flounder open, squelched out her roe, and began to examine each egg.

"What are you doing?" Loki asked him.

"Minding my own business," said the troll.

Then the troll found the egg he was looking for. "Third time lucky!" he grunted, and he smiled a horrible, twisted smile.

"What is it?" Loki asked.

"What does it look like?" the troll replied. "An egg."

"Show me."

The troll showed Loki the single egg, lying pale pink on the tip of his coarse forefinger, and as fast as a licking flame the Trickster snatched it . . .

Yes, Loki snatched it, and there was Asta! There she was, standing between Loki and the mountain-troll.

The troll roared.

"Quick!" Loki urged the little girl. "Quick as quick! Hide in your father's boatshed."

Asta light-footed it over the loose pebbles, scampered over the scrub, and fairly threw herself into the boatshed, slamming the rickety door behind her.

The troll was only a few yards behind. He wrenched the door off its hinges, peered into the gloom, and bellowed at Asta to come out.

Come out? That's the last thing Asta meant to do.

The troll bent at the waist so that he could step into the shed. But a boatshed is much smaller than a longhouse, and he smashed his forehead against the crossbeam right in front of him.

The troll tottered sideways. Then he collapsed with a moan, and Loki bounded into the boatshed. He drew the troll's fishing knife from his belt and slit his leathery throat.

Asta scooted out of the shed past the body of the troll. But before long she began to skip in the sunlight, and it seemed to her as if everything that had happened had been no more than strange, shape-shifting dreams.

What was it that Odin the Allfather, greatest of the gods, had said? "What I can do I have done. But the time comes when here on Middle Earth each man must help himself and each woman help herself."

And shining Honir, the peacemaker? "What I can do I have done. But now you must help yourselves."

Loki, though, the Trickster, not only did he outwit the mountain-troll, but he put an end to him and saved Asta's life.

That's why Ulf and Thora were in no doubt, in no doubt whatsoever, that Loki was the greatest of all the gods and goddesses in Asgard.

———

SKARP'S GHOST

---

*The twins were always playing
tricks on each other. As they were
walking through the graveyard one
night, Something sat up. And the
Something said, "Isn't it fun
to play in the dark?"*

A fair old crowd rode in for Skarp's funeral,

not because they liked him, not one bit, but they admired his widow Gudrun and knew what a kind and generous woman she was. It was harvest month, and so Gudrun was able to feed her guests with fresh meat and wheatcakes, and her newly brewed ale soon loosened many tongues.

"A skinflint and a miser."

"He would have fed us leavings and cold porridge."

"She should have divorced him—he beat her black-and-blue."

What's certain is that during the night after Skarp was buried in his hole, no one saw the sky open so that the sky-spirits could shine their flaming torches and guide Skarp up along the pathway to join them.

Everyone at the funeral was very surprised when his widow told them she couldn't find any of Skarp's money. Not so much as a single silver coin. Gudrun said she and the five laborers who worked on the farm had turned everything over in the fire hall, and even raised the floorboards and stuck their knives into the turf wall, and searched the sheds and stables.

"He must have taken it all with him," one neighbor asserted.

"That's what he did," another agreed. "He hid all his money before he died."

"And he'll be back for it," warned a third man.

Well, September soon came on, and Skarp did come back. Before long, his ghost was walking almost every night. It walked out of the graveyard and right into the farm, moaning and kind of whistling wherever it went, and opening creaking doors and thumping the low beams in the fire hall.

The ghost kept waking Gudrun's five laborers, and most times they couldn't get back to sleep, so they all decided to leave the farm as soon as the long winter darkness came to an end and to look for work elsewhere. And that's what they did.

I'll have to sell the farm, Gudrun thought. *I can't run it on my own. I'll have to sell it.* She gave a heartfelt sigh. *Skarp! You were bad alive, and now you're even worse dead!*

But just before the flitting days at the end of May, a laborer no one recognized walked into the farm and offered to work for Gudrun.

"I've heard how things are," he told the widow, "and I'll help you. We can turn things around."

Gudrun wasn't quite sure why—maybe it was just that she so much wanted to—but she believed the man, and there and then she hired him.

"Tell me," the laborer asked her, "did your husband have a large amount of money?"

Gudrun raised her shoulders and shook her head. "I really don't know. We searched everywhere."

The laborer—his name was Gardar—helped Gudrun to haul out sacks of barley from her barn into the home field and to sow it there.

"Better late than never," he said.

And then, as Cuckoo Month ended and Egg Time began, they worked side by side, helping the ewes with their lambing. True, they couldn't care for every corner of the large farm in the way that Skarp's five laborers had been able to do, but they worked their fingers to the bone—cutting peat and chopping wood for the fire, spreading manure, mending fences.

Just before the summer solstice, when the sun never set but mysteriously seemed to hang, almost to bounce on the western horizon before rising again, Gardar rode to market. He wasn't able to buy much, because Gudrun had very little silver to buy anything with, but he did come back with two purchases of his own. One was a sheet of iron, and the other was a sheet of linen, the color of oatmeal, the kind that people used to wind around corpses.

When he got back to the farm, Gardar sewed the linen into a shroud and then he lit a fire and got to work on the sheet of iron. He wasn't the best blacksmith in the world, but he wasn't the worst, and he was able to forge for himself a breastplate and a pair of gauntlets, to cover the back of his hands and fingers.

The next night, Gardar tied on the breastplate and gauntlets and wrapped himself in the shroud. Then he went over to the graveyard and up to Skarp's grave, and there he walked to and fro, tossing a piece of hacksilver from one palm to the other.

A white and gray column, thin as smoke, rose from Skarp's grave. It quivered a little and somehow assembled itself.

Then it drifted over to Gardar.

"One of us, are you?" it asked in a trembling voice.

"As you see," the laborer whispered in a ghostly kind of way.

"Let me touch you," said Skarp's ghost.

So Gardar held out his left iron gauntlet, and the ghost could feel how bloodless and cold it was.

"What are you walking for?" it murmured.

"To play with my money," the laborer whispered.

"What? Just one piece?" jeered the ghost, and it gave a hollow laugh. "One piece! Follow me."

Then Skarp's ghost drifted over the graveyard wall, and the laborer scrambled after it, taking great care not to scratch and scrape his breastplate or gauntlets on the rough stone. At the very top of the home field there were several tussocks and soft hummocks, and from one Skarp's ghost unearthed a wooden box full of pieces of silver—coins, rings, and little brooches, and dozens of odds and ends of hacksilver.

When he saw them, Gardar gasped and raised both his hands, and the ghost laughed an airy gloating laugh that seemed never to end but simply became one with the soft night.

For hour after hour the ghost amused itself by turning over each piece of shining silver and stacking it all up, arranging it, then rearranging it.

"How often do you come here?" Gardar asked the ghost.

"Every night. I check my silver's all here and play with it and count it and recount it."

The sun was just lowering herself onto the horizon. The light around Gardar and Skarp's ghost was gloomy; the air was very, very still.

The ghost sighed an unearthly sigh.

"Time to hide it all away again," it breathed. "Soon it will be dawn."

"One more game," whispered Gardar. "Just the hacksilver."

But then the laborer grasped a whole handful of the chips and splinters and shavings of silver and tossed them up so that they fell all over the place like confetti.

"What are you doing?" the ghost demanded. "You're not a ghost."

"I am," protested Gardar in a hoarse voice. "Of course I am. Feel my right hand."

The ghost felt the laborer's right gauntlet, cold with the cold of night, and was reassured. Then it gathered all the silver and put it back into the box. But Gardar, he grabbed the box and tipped the whole lot out again.

The ghost screamed.

"What are you doing? You're not a ghost."

"Feel," said the laborer.

So the ghost clutched him and felt Gardar's cold iron breastplate. It sniffed and moaned. "Yes," it murmured. "We are the same."

After this, Gardar didn't dare to take any more risks. Instead, he asked the ghost whether he could add his own piece of hacksilver to the chest.

"To keep it safe," he said. "I'm always afraid of losing it, and I've only got one piece."

"Just one piece!" scoffed the ghost, and then it gave a kind of laugh and added Gardar's hacksilver to its box.

After they had got back to the graveyard, the ghost quivered and asked Gardar, "Your hole. Where is it?"

"Oh!" said Gardar. "Over there, on the other side."

"It is, is it? Well, you go first."

"No, no," moaned the laborer, "you go into your hole first."

The laborer and Skarp's ghost began to argue, but time was against the ghost. The sun started to lift from the blue horizon, day dawned, and it had no choice but jump back into its grave.

As soon as Gardar got back to the farm, he rolled one of the casks that had been emptied of ale at Skarp's funeral into the fire hall. Then he levered up three of the floorboard planks and lowered the cask into it.

With Gudrun's help, he filled the cask almost to the brim with water from the stream running past the farm, and he dropped into it his iron breastplate and gauntlets and his linen shroud.

Then Gardar went back on his own to the top of the homefield. Swiftly he dug into the soft earth of the hummock, picked up the heavy wooden chest with the silver inside it, and carried it back to the farm.

First he showed all the silver to Gudrun, and then he lowered the chest into the cask on top of the breastplate and gauntlets and linen shroud, and although it was made of wood, the cask sank because of the weight of all the silver inside it.

The long day passed, and as usual Gudrun went to her own bed-closet—a little wood-paneled room at one end of the hall—while Gardar lay down on a mattress next to the locked door and the cask underneath the floorboards.

At much the same time as Gardar had gone out to the graveyard on the previous night, Skarp's ghost came drifting into the fire hall, searching for its treasure chest. It passed right through the locked door and started to peer and pry and sniff into every corner.

But because the laborer had covered his clothing and the treasure chest with water, the ghost was unable to smell any earth still clinging to them.

Skarp's ghost stood over the laborer. It stooped and gave the floorboards an almighty thump—exactly what with, only the old gods could say—so that they screeched.

Then the ghost moaned and sort of twisted and slid out the fire hall again. At once the laborer got up and followed it, and he didn't come back until he was sure that it had gone down into its hole.

Next morning, Gardar returned to Skarp's grave carrying a spade and a pickaxe. He began to dig and dig until he had dug up the farmer's body. He never told anyone exactly what he did with it, but he manhandled it in such a horrible way that Skarp's ghost never rose out of its hole again.

Well, everyone living for miles around admired Gardar for the way he had tricked the ghost, but none more so than Skarp's widow, Gudrun.

She married him, and their farm prospered.

And that's the end of the story.

———

BLUE
OF BLUE

---

*Blue? Blue, it's next
to Always.*

It was the week

when Inga and Arni and their parents and their neighbors knew once more that they lived a little nearer to Asgard than anyone else on Middle Earth.

The first week in June, when there was light, light everywhere, light all day and almost all night. It was when the mist-scarfs lifted early and vanished into the cool air. When hopes were high and hearts and tongues sang.

Bloody-bones and specters and scrats and sendings and wizards, they all lay low, and Inga and her younger brother made wreaths of wildflowers and hung them round the necks of their cattle. Then they drove them past the ponds, stinking of sulfur, and past the broken ground where the earth was seething and columns of steam rose into the sky; they walked their cattle and seventeen sheep and their one wicked goat all the way up to the high mountain pastures.

The family owned their own wooden hut up there, and that's where they lived for the summer months, herding and milking each day, making butter and skyr and soft cheese.

On the first night, Inga stayed there alone to watch over the animals while Arni went back down to help his parents, Harald and Aud, carry up a whole assortment of objects—wooden bowls and basins and pails and sewing frames and two stools and bedding and a little harp and the high skies know what else!

Before she lay down, Inga prayed as she always did to the goddess Frigg to watch over her, and then she slept. And soon after the sun started to climb again, she was on her feet before she realized she was awake, and out of the door before she realized she was still barefoot. She felt so eager, so fresh, so impatient.

Inga tousled her flaxen hair; she looked out and about with her bright blue eyes.

She knew that nothing was impossible. Nothing!

But this was when she realized that Shabby, their goat, had slipped her halter.

She looked up, she looked away across the green slopes, she looked down. Then Inga peered up again, and there Shabby was, standing right at the very top of the pasture beneath the awkward black ribs of the mountain.

"Shabby!" shouted Inga. "Shabby! Come down!"

But the goat had not the slightest intention of doing anything of the kind. She stood stock-still and dared Inga to follow her. She didn't even shake her beard.

"Shabby!" cried Inga as she began to plod up toward her. "I know what you'll do. Why am I even trying to catch you?"

And then, rather out of breath, "This isn't turning out the way I wanted."

Not as Inga wanted, and not as she could possibly have imagined.

Following Shabby, Inga came to a very steep green glade guarded by black rock. The moment she stepped onto the luscious grass, she felt sure it was a place where no one in Midgard had ever stepped before.

It was so still, so quiet that she could hear the sound of the grass growing.

Inga forgot about Shabby. She forgot about her cattle and sheep and the whole world below. She climbed up the green glade until she reached the gritty white claws of a glacier, shining so fiercely that she had to look at it between her fingers.

Then Inga saw that only a little way up the icy slope, there was a fissure, a kind of dark scar.

Still barefoot, Inga got down onto her hands and knees and pulled herself up, up, and over a hump until she was kneeling at the mouth of a cave.

The roof and walls and floor of the cave were lit by an unearthly blue ice-light. In one place they were dazzling, in another very dark, but for the most part they shone with a pearly sheen.

Inga saw a woman standing in the middle of the cave. She was dressed wholly in white, and Inga knew at once that it was Frigg because she had seen the goddess in her dreams.

Just behind her stood four young women. They were all wearing chaplets and chokers of wildflowers, and all smiling.

This is Frigg's palace here in Midgard, thought Inga. *She usually lives in Asgard, and I know Odin's her husband, but sometimes she comes down to Midgard when she wants to favor human beings.*

"Inga," the goddess greeted her. "Welcome!"

Inga fell to her knees, but Frigg gestured to her to stand up again. Then she saw the goddess was holding a bunch of little blue flowers in her right hand.

"As blue as your eyes," Frigg told her with an airy smile.

The four young women stepped forward, and each of them lightly touched the top of Inga's head and blessed her.

Inga looked up and then round, and she realized the cave's uneven roof and walls were decorated with hundreds and hundreds of rubies and emeralds and opals and amethysts and mountain-stones. Some were arranged in simple patterns; some didn't look as if they'd been arranged at all.

"Inga," said the goddess, "you may choose whatever you like from this cave. You can take it home with you."

Inga drew in her breath and looked round the cave again. She knew that even a little handful of jewels would make her poor family rich for many years, but all the same she kept having another look at Frigg's bunch of little blue flowers.

They're not just blue but the spirit of blue, she thought. *Blue of blue . . . They're alive, they're breathing, and the goddess Frigg has held them in her own right hand. But the emeralds and rubies and opals and that, they're all cold and stone-dead.*

"If you'll let me . . ." Inga began, and she kept her head lowered because she didn't quite dare to look into the goddess's eyes. "If you'll let me, I'd like to take your flowers."

Frigg smiled. Gently she nodded. And Inga didn't see how her brilliant blue eyes were filled with love and laughter.

"Yes," declared the goddess. "The right words. The right choice."

Inga realized she was quite out of breath, and each time she breathed she was making a balloon of air.

"For as long as these flowers bloom," the goddess told her, "your family's farm will be fruitful. But when they lose their color and shrivel, so will you, Inga. Take these flowers and this pouch full of seeds. Sow them in the field below your farm, and tend them as they grow. Take them now."

So Inga took the bunch of flowers and did look into the goddess's eyes. And the moment she did, she was dazzled and for a moment blinded by Frigg's brightness.

When she could see again, she was standing outside the crystal cave with the bunch of flowers in one hand and the pouch of seeds in the other. And Shabby was standing there too, twitching her beard and staring at her.

■ ■ ■

"You idiot!" wailed Inga's mother when she and her husband and Arni reached the shieling and heard Inga's story.

"Idiot!" Arni repeated gleefully.

"Are you telling me that you chose that bunch of flowers when you could have had a fistful of jewels?"

Inga looked defiantly at her mother.

"Didn't you stop to think? Look at them, Inga. They're already wilting."

"They're not."

Inga's mother fingered one of the misty, delicate blossoms. "Very strange they are, too," she said suspiciously. "I've never seen the likes of them before."

"Let the girl be," Inga's father told his wife, and he opened the pouch of seeds. "If she really was Frigg . . ."

"She was," insisted Inga.

"Yes, and I'm a giantess and our cow jumped over the moon."

For as long as these flowers bloom, your family's farm will be fruitful . . .

Inga remembered the goddess's words and she wasn't quite sure where to put Frigg's flowers. In the end, she placed them in a wooden bucket of water just outside the door of the shieling, and next morning she and her father walked down to their farm and sowed all the seeds in a plot looking out across the valley.

When the two of them went down just seven days later, the plot was already covered with green shoots. And no more than a week after that, the yellowy stalks of the plants were as tall as Inga.

Then their little blue flowers opened, hundreds of them, thousands, a dream of them—delicate-veined and slightly trembling, each with eight or nine petals, misty.

"Your mother's right," Inga's father admitted. "Very strange. I've never seen the likes of them before."

Inga knew that she had never, never seen anything so beautiful.

Blue of blue.

Well, the summer weeks soon passed, and the time came for the family to usher all their cows and sheep and their wicked goat back down the mountainside from the shieling, and Inga carefully carried down the bunch of flowers Frigg had given to her and stood them on a sill in their farmhouse.

Early September. In the field, all the veined blue petals dropped, and the seed heads opened until they drooped, and all their leaves and stems paled and whitened and withered.

Very early one morning, while her father and Arni were still asleep, Inga and her mother went out to the shed to start milking the cows, and that was when Inga saw a woman was standing right beside the plot of land where she had planted the seeds. Yes, and there were four young women standing behind her.

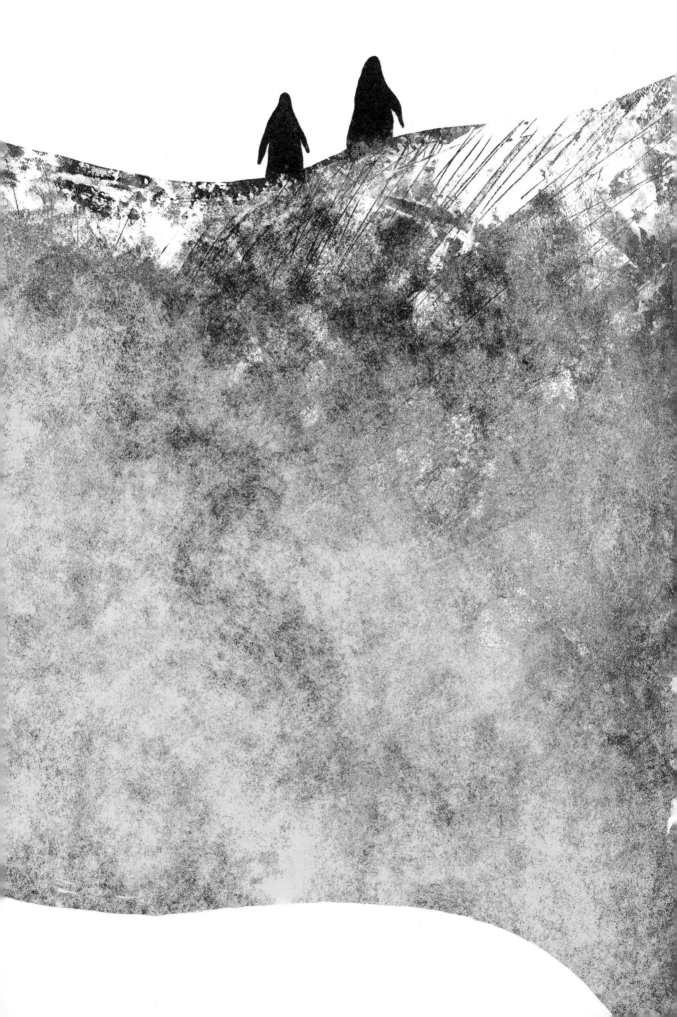

The woman was dressed entirely in white and wearing a gold girdle, and at once Inga dropped to her knees.

Her mother didn't quite know what to do. She covered her mouth, then her face; she inclined her head and sort of bowed and awkwardly got down onto her knees.

"Inga," the goddess began, "I see how well you've looked after the seeds I gave you. So now I've come down to show you what to do with the stalks."

"The stalks!" muttered Inga's mother.

"And if you do as I say," the goddess continued, "you and your mother, you'll grow rich."

"For as long as . . ." Inga whispered.

"Yes," breathed Frigg, and she smiled at Inga with her brilliant blue eyes.

Then the goddess helped Inga's mother to her feet. "This plant is called flax," she explained, "and each September you must collect the seed heads ready to sow next year."

Inga could see that her mother wanted to say something, as she always did, but she was too nervous to open her mouth.

"Don't cut the stalks," Frigg warned them, "or you'll lose the sap inside them. Pull the plants right out of the earth."

Inga nodded.

"Ripple them with a comb and remove all their seed heads. And then soak them in a tub of water so the stalks come apart from the fiber inside them."

Again Inga nodded.

"And then," the goddess went on, "comb the fibers as you comb your long hair."

Inga smiled a little smile. "Sometimes!" she said.

"Then you can wind them onto a bobbin," Frigg told Inga and her mother, "and spin with them. And what you spin with the fibers is called linen. It feels cool in summer and warm in winter—the finest of all fabrics."

Inga's mother shook her head. "Well, I never!" she exclaimed.

"Remember everything I've told you," the goddess cautioned them, "and remember my words are for your ears only."

Then Frigg blessed them both, and she and her four young attendants simply vanished. One moment they were there, and the next they were not. Inga and her mother were standing alone again in the soft, early morning light.

Each June, Inga and her family planted the flaxseeds they had carefully collected the previous autumn. And each summer the green shoots grew, and their plot of land turned blue of blue.

Inga and her mother spun more and more linen, her father sold it at a good price at the great October market, and the family was able to buy more fields and sow them as well with flaxseeds.

Inga married, and she had four children, and each of them married and had their own children. She shared with them all the secrets she had learned from the goddess, and together they became the most prosperous family in the district.

Each and every morning, Inga glanced at the bunch of blue flax flowers standing on a sill in the farmhouse—the flowers still as fresh as on the day when Frigg had given them to her so many years before, when she had been a girl.

One day, though, she saw that they were drooping, and by the next day they were hanging their heads, no longer as bright as before.

But when they lose their color and shrivel, so will you, Inga.

She knew it was almost time for her to die.

I must go back, she thought. *Back to that high ice cave, and I must get down on my poor old knee bones and thank the goddess.*

Without telling her children or her children's children where she was going, Inga plodded back up the pasture to their shieling, and then up to the black ribs of the mountain.

There she stood for a while to regain her breath, and remembered how she had followed Shabby across the slopes, and how their wicked goat had never once obeyed her for as long as she lived.

Inga stepped into the steep green glade and onto the claw of the glacier. On her hands and knees, she pulled herself into the dark mouth of the cave.

Blue ice-light . . . dazzling . . . very dark . . .

"Inga! Welcome!"

The goddess Frigg and her four young attendants were standing there, all of them wearing chaplets and chokers of wildflowers, as if not a day, not one moment, had passed since Inga had entered the cave all those years before.

"Welcome!" the goddess said again with a gentle smile. "We've been waiting for you."

Old Inga bent down and pressed the palms of her hands against the ground and lowered herself onto her knees, but at once Frigg stepped forward and raised her to her feet again.

"Come and live with me now in Fensalir—my hall in Asgard. I will always care for you."

Inga closed her faded blue eyes.

And here, in Midgard, she was never seen or heard of again.

YOUR
LIFE OR
MY LIFE

*Greetings! I've heard just
how wise you are. So you
know everything?*

When there was a strange crackling in the sky-dome, or sudden flashes, or bellowing, people down in Midgard knew that the gods and goddesses were angry and arguing, or so restless they could scarcely bear their own company, let alone that of anyone else.

And the gods were never more restless than near the end of the long, long dark winter, when they had been cooped up for months, and still it seemed as if spring would never arrive.

Religiously, each of them ate one of Idun's apples as soon as they woke each morning, but by noon they were often flushed and hectic and quick-tempered.

Heaven fever! That's what they were all suffering from.

Odin sat in Hlidskjalf, the high seat in his hall, and gazed out over the nine worlds. Pink and gray and violet and pale green they were, as the light of spring promised to return, and Allfather's head and heart were filled with an almighty longing.

"Early tomorrow," he announced, "I'll cross the rainbow bridge. I long to be in Midgard. I long to smell the first pale scents. I long to finger the first blades of grass and hear the thin bleating of the first wobbly lambs. I long to taste—"

"Be patient," his wife Frigg counseled him. "It is not yet spring."

"Tomorrow," insisted Odin. "Midgard again! And then I'll cross the river that never freezes, and climb up to the cave of that wise rock-giant, and test my wits against his wits."

"Tangler!" exclaimed Frigg. "He knows more than Mimir and more than Hyndla. More than any other giant or giantess."

"And I know more than him," asserted Odin. "There may be things I can learn from him, but I'll be able to outwit him."

Wearing his long, dark blue cloak and wide-brimmed hat, one-eyed Odin crossed Bifrost into sleeping Midgard, and at once he sensed and remembered things he hadn't even thought of since the previous autumn: the way the stately pine trees huddled so close together for company and whispered to each other; how the wild geese flew in arrowheads and their leader kept squawking instructions; how, when there was a sprinkling of snow, the moon himself shone so brightly that he could make a rainbow.

It was too early for anyone to be up and about. On late winter mornings, everyone huddled and cuddled indoors, in their little bed-closets or around the fire.

Not that Odin cared much. Not, in fact, that he cared at all. True, he sometimes helped people in trouble, as he'd helped Ulf and Thora when the troll threatened to take their daughter, Asta. But more often he was indifferent, and sometimes he was cruel.

"There are three classes of people," Allfather said, "slaves and peasants and warriors. Some die in childbirth, some live short lives, some long, but they all die when they're fated to die. That's how things are."

Odin himself sometimes cut humans down like corn when they got in his way: farmhands working in the fields, rivals for the favors of a lovely girl, warriors in battle. And he well knew that although men and women and children were scared of him, and worshipped him, they didn't care much for him either, and gave him many fearsome names: Terrible One, Father of Battle, Bringer of Sleep, Spear-Shaker, Death-Blinder, Allfather.

But they knew too that Odin would live until the end of the world.

■ ■ ■

After he had waded across the river called Iving, Odin hurried over the rocky slopes and up to the cave of the rock-giant, Tangler.

In front of the cave, a wicked army of rock slabs were standing upright, or leaning against each other, or piled on top of each other, so that it would have been quite impossible to ride up to the cave's dark mouth.

Allfather picked his way through them and strode straight into the cave. And as soon as he made out the giant, sitting in the gloom in his high-backed seat, he called out, "Greetings, giant."

"Tangler," replied the giant. "That's my name."

"I've heard about you," Odin said, "and how you confuse men and muddy their minds."

"What about you?" asked Tangler. "Who are you?"

"I'm the one who knows the way," Odin said with a slow, arrogant smile. "I'm Gagnrad."

"The one who knows the way," Tangler mocked him. "Well, we'll see about that. No one has ever escaped with his life from my cave."

"After a long journey," Odin said, "a guest expects courtesy and a tumbler of ale, not a mouthful of threats."

"Quite right," agreed Tangler. "You've no need to stand. Sit down. Help yourself to some ale. And then . . . we'll find out who knows more."

But Odin ignored the giant. He stepped nearer to him and remained on his feet.

"All right," Tangler said. "Stand if you want to. What's the name of the stallion . . . the stallion who pulls Day's chariot across the sky?"

Odin smiled. "Skinfaxi," he replied. "Skinfaxi with his shining mane."

"All right," Tangler said. "Stand if you want to. What's the name of the stallion who rides in from the east, pulling Night behind him?"

"Hrimfaxi," answered the god. "Each dawn, lashings and globs of foam fall from his bit, and that's why there's dew down in the valleys."

"All right, Gagnrad. Stand if you want to. What's the river called that streams between the world of the gods and the world of the giants?"

"Iving," Odin replied. "It has never once frozen over, and it never will."

"All right, Gagnrad," said Tangler. "Stand if you want to. What's the name of the huge plain where all the giants, led by Surt the fire-giant, will fight with the gods before the world ends?"

"Vigrid," answered Odin. "It's at least a hundred miles long and a hundred miles wide."

From somewhere deep in the cave, there was a nasty clatter.

"Nothing but a rockfall," Tangler told his guest with a grim smile. "There's no need to be frightened." He stared thoughtfully at Odin, but the god kept his head bowed. "Well, you know more than I thought you would," the giant told him. "Come now! Sit down. Pour yourself a tumbler of ale, and put me some questions."

So Odin sat down.

"Your head . . . or my head . . ." Tangler intoned very slowly. "What do you say?"

Odin nodded.

"Yes," growled Tangler. "Your life . . . or my life. We'll wager our lives on who wins this contest."

"First, tell me then, Tangler: Our earth and sky, where did they come from?"

Tangler filled his cheeks and blasted a tide of foul breath into his guest's face. "Our earth was molded from the frost-giant Ymir's body. The mountains are his bones. The salt seas and oceans are his blood. As for the sky: well, the sky-dome above the nine worlds is Ymir's skull."

"Second, Tangler. Where did you and all your giants come from? Who were your first ancestors?"

"The river called Elivagar is often wild," Tangler replied. "Once, it began to spew poison. The drops of poison began to clot, just as blood clots. And the clot took the shape of a giant called Ymir. That's where we come from, Gagnrad, and why we're all so fierce."

"Very good," agreed Odin, and he gulped a swig of ale. "But if this giant, Ymir, never slept with a giantess, how was he able to have children?"

"Ha!" exclaimed Tangler. "Hot and wet! A boy grew in his left armpit, and a girl in his right armpit. And then . . ." Tangler paused and smiled. "With his left leg, Ymir fathered a son on his right leg. A son with six heads."

Gagnrad nodded, and he sighed. "Tell me this, Tangler. We hear it, soothing, whistling, trumpeting. It shakes the grass, it whips up the waves, but we never see it. So where does wind come from?"

"At the end of the world," Tangler replied, "sits the eagle Hraesvelg, the Corpse-Eater. Whenever he flaps his huge wings, he stirs the air into wind."

"First you asked me four questions," Odin told the giant, "and now I've asked you four. This time, it's my turn to begin."

Tangler nodded.

"Who are the men in Odin's hall," Allfather asked him, "the men who go out to fight each morning?"

"It's said that all the dead heroes in Odin's hall go out to fight each morning," answered Tangler. "They go out and fight again, they're killed again, and yet their wounds soon heal, and they feast together each evening."

Gagnrad smiled. "Is that so? I've heard that after the gods and giants and all creation meet in battle, there will be the most terrible winter—a winter such as there has never been. So what will survive it?"

Tangler nodded again. "A young man and young woman will hide themselves inside Yggdrasill, the tree that reaches over the nine worlds and guards us all. The dew that settles each dawn on its leaves will nourish them."

"Third, Tangler, this. I've heard Odin will be killed at the great battle on the Plain of Vigrid. Do you know how?"

"I do," the giant replied. "Fenrir the wolf will break free from his chains and swallow Odin." He gave Gagnrad a long, thoughtful look.

"Whatever the gods know, I know," the giant's guest declared. He swilled more ale around his mouth. "When his dead son Balder had been placed on his funeral pyre aboard his own ship, *Ringhorn* . . ."

Tangler nodded.

". . . his father Odin came aboard and bent over Balder. What did Odin whisper in his dead son's ear?"

For a very long time, the giant stared at his guest. He pursed his coarse lips and sucked his cheeks and chewed on them.

If anyone had been watching, it might have seemed to them that they'd been watching Odin and the giant ask each other riddles for many hours, and had to wait even longer now for Tangler to reply.

"I cannot tell," Tangler growled in a low voice. "No one in the nine worlds can tell what you, Odin, whispered in your son's ear. I've told you first things, I've told you last things, but from the beginning this was no contest, and you know it."

Allfather stood up.

"No one can pit himself against Odin and win," bellowed Tangler. "No one. You knew I was fated to die."

Odin parted his dark blue cloak and grasped Gungnir, his spear that never missed its mark. He pointed it straight at the rock-giant. He glared at Tangler with his one burning eye.

———

THE **GIFT** OF **POETRY**

---

*Who can be sure of living
after they have died?*

The boy gazed up at the pale fire in the northern night sky, and he watched while it kept changing shape—dragons and spears and green flames and warnings. He stared down at the stinking devil lake and the ground around it, the black sand and wasteland heaving and groaning. He looked at the columns of steam bursting from fissures and rising to Asgard.

He knew there were ghosts all over the place. Of course there were, what with the feuds and violent deaths of the past, and hurried burials without the right words or prayers, and what with buried treasure . . . and he knew you couldn't sleep easily on the nights when ghosts were walking.

The boy knew that there were trolls all around as well, and dwarfs and spirits. It was just that you couldn't see them, not unless they wanted you to. And he knew that from time to time gods and goddesses came down to Midgard to reward or punish someone, or lift them to everlasting life up in Asgard, or just when they were on their way to somewhere else— the wide ocean surrounding Midgard, or the mountainous home of the frost-giants and rock-giants, or misty Niflheim, nine days' ride northward and downward from Midgard, where Hel ruled over the dead.

The boy was called Aran, and he knew the nine worlds were beautiful and terrible.

I was that boy.

■ ■ ■

I lived with my mother and father and Helga, my young sister, in a lap of green land at the very foot of a hill. Whenever I climbed the hill, I could see some of its white bones where the turf had withered and died away.

From the top I could easily make out all the mountains stretched out along the skyline, like a giant's sleeping body I used to think. But sometimes there was a dust storm and my whole world blurred. It got inside my head and muddled all my thoughts.

I can hear it now—that soft whistling of the little stand of birch trees next to our longhouse. Then I'd rub my eyes and see how they discovered themselves again, slender and silver, as the whirling dust storm blew away.

Sometimes, our friend Halldor rode over from his farm to visit us— and those were the best times. It is said that he was a distant cousin of ours, but that's no surprise, because everyone here in Iceland is related to one another.

Halldor couldn't pluck his harp with his toes and send poisonous snakes to sleep, like people say that the great poet Gunnar did, and he wasn't so fine a harpist that he could make wooden mugs and dishes dance at a midday feast. But when he sat down at our fireside and took his little harp out of his leather bag, my heart beat faster.

And when he began to sing, to sing-and-say, with that rich voice of

his . . . when he sang his own poems about heroes and lovers and feuds and shape-changers and all the unseen beings around us, my head and heart were filled with such flames, such fears and longings.

Because of Halldor, I knew each waterfall was alive, each column of steam and plume of cloud, each birch leaf and rowan leaf, each moonwort and spotted orchid. They were alive and I shared their lives and longings.

When I was a boy, I wanted to be like Halldor, and told him I wanted to learn the rules and skills of poetry.

"The god Bragi taught me," he said, "as he teaches each poet, and if it's his wish, I will teach you."

But! By the time I was eleven, the bright world I lived in . . . somehow it began to fade, as a bright day does well before the sun slips below the horizon.

From season to season, my father gave me more duties on our farm. I learned to shear sheep. I learned to scythe and toss and turn grass and mend stone walls to keep foxes and bears out from our barley and oats, and to walk over to the screeching and shrieking sea cliffs at Egg Time and come back with baskets of eggs.

I learned all these things, but what interested me most was myself, my growing body, and girls—ah! girls—and clouds of airy nonsense about time and sin and space and love.

I often felt tired. So tired. When I wasn't up and out and about, working on our land, many times I stretched out by the firepit.

My mother grumbled but she understood.

Halldor didn't ride over nearly so often then, partly because he'd broken both his legs when his horse threw him and they were always painful and never mended right; but perhaps also because I, Aran, was no longer so eager to learn from him, so insistent.

But as soon as he began to pluck his harp and sing . . . his notes and songs were stepping-stones. Halldor's stories and songs gave me back my first bright belonging.

But then Halldor died. One day he clutched his heart and cried out; he died before he had taught me the rules and skills of poetry.

"The god Bragi taught me . . . and if it's his wish, I will teach you."

I felt part of my own self had died with Halldor. But I also knew I had to be all the more alive, alive to myself and everyone and everything, because he had gone.

We all rode over to Halldor's farm and his family buried him there.

Everyone in the district gathered around his earth mound. We told

stories about him and remembered things he'd said, and we laughed and wept. We remembered him.

That was when I knew that, more than anything, I wanted to sing-and-say my own praise-poem for Halldor, even though he had never taught me the rules and skills of poetry.

Slowly the mourners dispersed. People rode off, north and south, east and west. The stars began to burn, and the lion came leaping across the sky. I told my mother and father and Helga that I would follow them.

I spread my cloak and lay down in the dew beside Halldor's mound.

And while I was trying to link at least a few words in the right way in praise of Halldor, I seemed to fall asleep.

Then the side of the earth mound opened and, dressed in his white burial-sheet, Halldor softly walked out. He came right up to me and stood over me.

"Aran," he said in his rich voice, "I know why you're here. And I know how much you long to be a poet.

"As you know, the mead of poetry was made by dwarfs—they mixed the blood of the magician Kvasir with honey. But the giants stole it from the dwarfs, and then Odin our Allfather won it back from the giants. And now, from time to time, Odin allows a man or woman to sip the mead and become a poet. Not only that, he allows poets to pass on their gift to another young man or woman if they choose to do so."

Halldor paused.

"I am willing," he told me, "to give you the gift of poetry if you are able to receive it."

The night air felt very cool. My brow and my face were burning.

"It's no disgrace to try but to fail," Halldor said. "The dishonor is not to dare to try, and I've never heard it said that to be a poet is an easy calling. It's testing and demanding. Learning all the rules about syllables and stresses and rhyme and half-rhyme and alliteration, that's hard work. And fulfilling them, that's never in the least easy. As for finding the true words, the true music of memory and praise—so as to honor the dead and to delight the living—that's the most difficult task of all."

Again Halldor paused. "There's no dishonor in being a farmer," he said. "Or a fisherman. None at all.

"But I see how restless you are. I see how willing, how eager. So this is your test, Aran. I will tell you this verse, and you must remember it, and never share it with anyone, not until your turn comes to share your gift.

"If in the morning you've forgotten it, think of our meeting as a dream, and go home to your parents and your sister, your farm. But if you remember it, then you have made your choice. You must work at learning and honoring and delighting, and you will become a poet."

Halldor touched the tip of my tongue with his right forefinger, and it tasted rich and sweet. In that way, he put the verse in my mind.

"I will remember the verse," I told him.

The old poet drew himself up and raised his eyes to Asgard. Then he turned away and, dressed in his white burial-sheet, walked back into his earth mound.

I lay down again on my cloak beside the mound. I slept there until the sky lightened and brightened.

The moment I opened my eyes, the first words of the verse were on my honey-sweet tongue.

I mouthed them, and then I sang them out:

Poet, life-pilgrim, Halldor,

word-weaver, that's who you were.

And you now, Aran, apprentice . . .

■ ■ ■

But even now, after so many years, I cannot share the whole verse with anyone, not until my turn comes to pass this holy gift on to whoever is ready to receive it.

Will that be you?

Will it be your tongue I touch with the mead of poetry? And you to whom I'll say:

Poet, life-pilgrim, Aran,

word-weaver, that's who you were.

And you now . . .

The author wishes to acknowledge the wonderful team at Walker Books, and especially my incomparable editor Denise Johnstone-Burt, her eagle-eyed assistant Louisa Dinwiddie, and my superb and sensitive art editor Ben Norland: very, very many thanks. Warm thanks, too, to Karen Clarke, who deciphered my manuscript, Lynda Edwards-Evans for her advice on flax, and my wife Linda for her loving support and close readings of many drafts of each tale. Lastly, gratitude to Jeffrey Alan Love, whose thrilling illustrations if anything exceed the drama and power of those in *Norse Myths*, our first book together.

Text copyright © 2020 by Kevin Crossley-Holland. Illustrations copyright © 2020 by Jeffrey Alan Love. • All rights reserved. No part of this book may be reproduced, transmitted, or stored in an information retrieval system in any form or by any means, graphic, electronic, or mechanical, including photocopying, taping, and recording, without prior written permission from the publisher. • First US edition 2021. • Library of Congress Catalog Card Number pending. ISBN 978-1-5362-1771-1 • This book was typeset in Columbus and Imperfect. The illustrations were done in acrylic paint, ink, and pencil on board. • Candlewick Studio, an imprint of Candlewick Press, 99 Dover Street, Somerville, Massachusetts 02144. www.candlewickstudio.com Printed in Shenzhen, Guangdong, China. 21 22 23 24 25 26 CCP 10 9 8 7 6 5 4 3 2 1

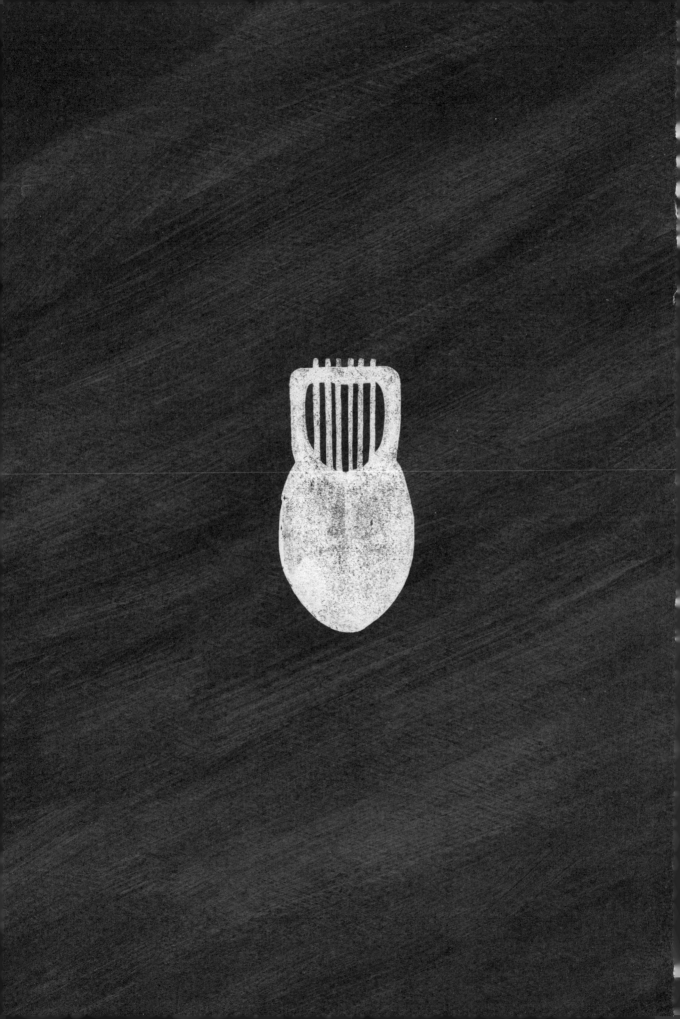